Disney's Princess Collection

Love & Friendship Stories

Ladybird

Table of Contents

TABLE OF CONTENTS

Written by Sarah E. Heller
Revised by Louisa Somerville
Designed by Todd Taliaferro

5 7 9 10 8 6 4

A Catalogue record for this book is available from the British
Library.

Printed by Ladybird Books Ltd
80 Strand
LONDON
WC2R 0RL

A Penguin Company

Ladybird and the device of a Ladybird are trademarks of Ladybird
Books Ltd.

Printed in Spain

WALT DISNEP'S

Cinderella

THE MICE SAVE THE DAY

Once there was a girl named Cinderella, who lived with her stepmother and her two stepsisters. They were jealous of Cinderella's charm and beauty and forced the poor girl to be a servant in her own home, sweeping the floor, cooking and carrying firewood.

"At least I have the birds and mice for friends," thought Cinderella.

One day, an invitation to the

Prince's ball arrived at the house. Cinderella's stepsisters were very excited. "The ball is tonight. We must get ready immediately!" they shrieked. "Cinderellllaa!" they yelled. "Mend our ballgowns, you lazy girl."

"Can I come to the ball too?" Cinderella asked anxiously.

"Only if you get all your work done!" her stepmother sneered, knowing that this was impossible.

Jaq, one of Cinderella's mouse friends, said, "Cinderella's not going to the ball." His friend Gus looked at him, startled. "She's only got her mother's old dress to wear, anyway!" he explained. "She'll never get her work done and mend the dress, too."

Just that day, Cinderella had rescued him from a mousetrap and mended his jacket. Jaq wanted to repay

her kindness. The mice decided to surprise her by

mending her dress. So, together with the birds, they lifted

ribbons and scissors and sewing needles to help make

Cinderella's dream come true.

"Oh, thank you so much!" the beautiful girl exclaimed when she saw what her friends had done for her. The birds and mice were overjoyed to see Cinderella so happy.

She deserved to have a special evening. However, it was not long before her stepmother and stepsisters took that hope away from her, too. When they saw Cinderella looking so lovely, they flew into a rage. Tearing her beautiful dress to shreds, they left poor Cinderella alone, sobbing in the garden.

"There, there," soothed a new voice. Cinderella's fairy godmother magically appeared. "Dry your tears," she said. "You can't go to the ball looking like that."

Cinderella started to explain that she wasn't going to

the ball, but her fairy godmother wouldn't hear of it.

Waving her magic wand, she turned a pumpkin into a

magnificent coach.

Cinderella stared at the magic in amazement. "Bibbidi

Bobbidi Boo!" sang the fairy godmother. Soon, four of the mice, including Jaq and Gus, were turned into horses.

As for Cinderella, her new gown shimmered like

diamonds. She stood staring at her image in the fountain with disbelief.

"It's more than I ever hoped for!" she declared, her eyes sparkling.

"Have fun at the ball," said her godmother. "But beware – the spell will

break at the stroke of midnight."

When she arrived at the palace, Cinderella was swept into a dream world. As she and the Prince swirled around the dance floor, everybody turned to stare at the beautiful girl who had caught the Prince's eye.

"Who is she?" they asked. "She must be a princess."

No one could have imagined that earlier that day she had been dressed in rags.

Never had Cinderella known such happiness! As the

handsome young Prince bowed before her, she felt her heart pounding. They danced together in the castle garden, swept up in the splendour of the evening.

Gazing into her eyes,

the Prince leaned to kiss her just as the clock struck twelve. When she heard the bell toll, Cinderella remembered her fairy godmother's warning. She raced down the grand staircase, leaving behind one of her dainty glass slippers.

The next day, the Prince sent the Grand Duke in search of the owner of the glass slipper. Realising that Cinderella was

the Prince's mysterious love, her stepmother mercilessly locked her in her room.

"No! Please let me out," cried Cinderella. She knew that the Grand Duke was trying the glass slipper on every maiden in the kingdom. He would be here soon.

"We've just got to get that key," Jaq told Gus. Despite the

danger, they pulled the key out of the stepmother's pocket,

then pushed and pulled it up the long staircase. With a last

burst of energy, Cinderella's exhausted little friends were

finally able to slip the key under her locked door.

Hurrying down the steps, Cinderella heard a crash. The

slipper she had left

behind was broken!

Pulling the other

slipper out of her

pocket, she called to the

Grand Duke, "May I

try this one on?"

The perfect fit proved that Cinderella was indeed the young woman who had won the Prince's heart.

Jaq and Gus cheered happily for their beautiful friend Cinderella as they watched her dreams come true.

Walt Disney's
Sleeping Beauty

THE FRIENDSHIP OF FAIRIES

In a magical kingdom, three kind and gentle fairies, named Flora, Fauna and Merryweather attended the christening of Princess Aurora. They brought special gifts of beauty, happiness and love to the baby.

Just as Merryweather raised her wand, there was a crack of thunder and Maleficent, the wicked fairy, stormed in. "I also have a gift," she hissed.

"Before sunset on your sixteenth birthday, you will prick your finger on the spindle of a spinning wheel and die!"

The king and queen were in despair, but just then Merryweather stepped forward. "I have not given my gift yet. Aurora won't die, but fall into a deep sleep, until a true love's kiss breaks the spell."

The three fairies offered to look after the child until her sixteenth birthday. Maleficent would never expect the fairies to live like peasants in the forest and raise the child themselves. Merryweather was reluctant to give up her wand.

"We've never done anything without magic before," she complained. But Flora insisted that they could do it if they worked together.

With love, they cared for the beautiful princess as if she were their own daughter. For fifteen years they kept her hidden in a cottage in the woods. Then, on the afternoon before her sixteenth birthday, the good

fairies sent Briar Rose, as they had named her, to pick berries so that they could plan a special surprise for her. Although they were sad about returning her to the king and queen at sunset, they wanted her to be happy.

Briar Rose sang as she gathered berries. She had the voice of an angel, and the squirrels and birds came to listen. She told them her dream of falling in love.

Nearby, Prince Phillip was riding his horse, Samson. Hearing Briar Rose's beautiful singing, he asked, "What do you think it is? A wood sprite, maybe?" He was so

entranced by her song that he promised Samson a carrot

if he would follow the music. The horse was so excited he

galloped too fast, knocking his friend off into a stream.

"No carrots for you!" said the Prince.

As he pulled himself out of the stream, the Prince caught sight of Briar Rose in a clearing in the wood, singing a love song to herself. He immediately fell in love

with her, but when he called out to her, she backed away. Prince Phillip called after her, "I'm not a stranger. We've met before."

He reminded her of the song she had been singing: "You said so yourself . . . 'once upon a dream.' "

Looking at him closely, Briar Rose felt that she really

did know him. His smile made her trust him, and she held his hand as they danced and walked through the magnificent forest. With a gentle touch and a tender look, they knew in a moment that this was a love as strong and true as one could ever be.

"This is the happiest day of my life," Briar Rose

proclaimed when she returned to the cottage. However,

Flora, Fauna and Merryweather were not pleased to hear

about her handsome stranger. As they explained that she

was a princess, Briar Rose fell into despair. She thought

that she would never see her love again.

Sadly, the fairies led the Princess to her castle home, but they didn't realise that Maleficent had discovered them and was waiting to carry out her curse. As Aurora pricked her finger on the spindle of the spinning wheel, she fell to the floor in a deep sleep.

Luckily, the good fairies soon discovered that Prince Phillip was the stranger Aurora had met in the woods. They realized that only his kiss could awaken the sleeping beauty.

They raced to Maleficent's castle to rescue him from her dungeon, where she had imprisoned him. The three fairies combined their powers of goodness in a fatal blow to the evil Maleficent, who had turned herself into a dragon.

"Sword of truth, fly swift and sure, that evil die and good endure." Their spell, combined with Prince Phillip's strength of heart, put an end to the wicked fairy.

Awakened by a tender kiss, Princess Aurora opened her eyes to behold the face of her true love. As Princess

Aurora and Prince Phillip expressed their love to the kingdom, the fairies danced with pleasure – knowing that their beautiful Briar Rose would live happily ever after.

Disney's

THE LITTLE MERMAID

PRINCESS OF THE SEA

Deep in the ocean, there lived a mermaid princess called Ariel, whose father, King Triton, forbade her to swim to the surface. One day, there was a storm at sea, and Ariel saw a handsome prince flung into the water from a ship. Disobeying her father, she swam quickly to the prince's rescue

and pulled him towards the shore.

As Ariel sang to him, his eyes opened. She gazed at the prince and fell deeply in love. Then she heard a voice. Quickly, she slipped back into the water, and watched from behind a rock as the prince's servant led him away.

King Triton wanted
Sebastian, Ariel's
music teacher, to keep
an eye on his youngest
daughter, and
Sebastian could not
disappoint the sea
king. He anxiously

tried to persuade Ariel that she would be happier under the

sea. "Down here is your home," he told Ariel, but despite

his efforts to make her understand the wonders of the

ocean, nothing could change her wish to be with the prince

because she had fallen deeply in love.

Only Flounder, Ariel's best friend, understood. Finding a statue of the prince that had gone down with the shipwreck, he surprised Ariel in her secret grotto.

"Flounder, you're the best!" she cried. "It looks just like him."

As she was imagining a romance with the prince, King Triton suddenly appeared. Seeing her

statue from the "barbarian" world above, he raised his

trident and smashed it to pieces, in a final attempt to protect

the princess from the dangers of the human world.

Ariel was so upset that she sought the help of the Sea

Witch, Ursula. "In exchange for your voice I will turn you into a human for three days," she said. "If the prince hasn't given you the kiss of true love in that time, you will become a mermaid again and belong to me forever."

Ariel was terrified but, thinking of the prince, she agreed.

A moment later she was walking on the seashore – a

human at last! It wasn't long before the prince, named Eric, arrived and noticed Ariel on a rock.

"You're the one!" he exclaimed. "The one I have been looking for!" Ariel nodded, but she couldn't talk. Eric remembered that the girl who had rescued him had the

most beautiful voice. "Oh, you couldn't be who I thought," he sighed.

Still, he invited her to the castle, and when they ate dinner together that night, Ariel made him laugh for the first time in weeks. The next day he took her on a tour of his kingdom, enchanted by her enthusiasm for everything from horses to puppet shows. She pulled him eagerly into a

dance, and she was thrilled when he let her take the reins

on the ride back to the castle. Surprised by her fun-loving

nature, Eric thoroughly enjoyed his new guest.

Sebastian decided to create a romantic mood that

evening as Ariel and Eric rowed together in a quiet lagoon. With soft music and moonlight on the water, the prince found himself

leaning forwards to kiss Ariel.

The Sea Witch had been watching, and fearing that her plan was about to fail, she sent a pair of eels to tip the boat over! The Sea Witch turned herself into a beautiful maiden

with Ariel's voice trapped in a seashell necklace around her

neck. Eric heard the voice and fell under its spell, and when

the witch asked him to marry her, he agreed.

All the ocean creatures gathered together to stall the

wedding while Flounder pulled Ariel to the ship. As her

friends tugged the shell from the witch's neck, Ariel's voice

was restored and the spell on Prince Eric was broken. He

ran to his true love, relieved that she had been the girl he wanted all along. But their kiss was too late – Ursula's three days had already ended. Ariel had become a mermaid once again, and the Sea Witch pulled her into the water.

"I lost her once. I'm not going to lose her again!" yelled Eric as he dived into the depths of the ocean. Using

strength, and the power of true love, the prince destroyed the Sea Witch. As he lay exhausted on the shore, Ariel watched him from afar.

Turning to Sebastian, King Triton asked, "She really does love him, doesn't she?" With tenderness, he granted his beautiful daughter her greatest wish. A few days later, Ariel married her prince. She finally knew true happiness.

Sebastian, Flounder and all the creatures of the sea applauded as Eric kissed his beautiful bride under a rainbow coloured with joy.

Disney's

Beauty and the Beast

FRIENDS IN STRANGE PLACES

Long ago, a traveller sought refuge in an enchanted castle owned by a Beast. The Beast threw the man in the dungeon. At last, the man's daughter, Belle, came looking for him. "Let me take my father's place," she

pleaded. The Beast agreed and sent the man on his way.

Belle discovered that the former servants of the castle had been turned into household objects. Mrs Potts, the teapot, and her son, Chip, a teacup, quickly put her at ease with their warmhearted welcome. "It'll turn out all right in the end, you'll see," soothed Mrs Potts.

Meanwhile, the Beast was nervous. An enchantress had changed him from a handsome prince into an ugly beast.

She had given him a magic rose and said, "If you learn to love and be loved before the last petal falls, the spell will be broken. If not, you will remain a Beast for ever."

The Beast had lost all hope until Belle arrived. Now he was

afraid that she would never see him as anything but a monster. "She's so beautiful and I'm . . . well, look at me!" he shouted to his servants.

"You must help her see past all that," Mrs Potts advised. She and Lumiere, a

candelabra, offered suggestions: act like a gentleman; compliment her; be gentle and sincere. "And above all," they said together, "you must control your temper!"

The Beast tried to be polite when he asked Belle to join him for dinner, but he was used to giving orders and

being obeyed. When Belle refused, he burst with anger and frustration. "If she won't eat with me, then she won't eat at all!" he roared.

Despite the master's orders, Mrs Potts would not let Belle go hungry. Instead she arranged a fantastic feast and Lumiere put on a show. The silver and china danced and they all sang together, "Be our guest!" Belle was happy and laughing. "That was wonderful!"

she exclaimed, clapping her hands.

Although she was fond of her new friends, Belle wanted nothing to do with the Beast. Only after he proved that he cared, by protecting her from wolves, did she begin to trust him. Slowly, a friendship developed.

One day, as they played in the snow, Belle watched the Beast feed the birds and realised there was a side of him that she hadn't seen before — a kind and gentle side.

The Beast was happy that Belle was no longer frightened of him. He wanted to give her a gift for bringing happiness back into his life. Covering her eyes, the Beast led her into the enormous library. Belle couldn't believe her eyes when she saw all of the books.

"They're yours,"

the Beast told her. He knew she loved books.

"Thank you so much!" she smiled.

As Belle read to the Beast, their friendship grew stronger. They could talk and laugh with each other as they could with no one else. Finally, a special evening was

planned. The Beast was worried. He wanted everything to be perfect, but he thought he could never be presentable. Cogsworth, the mantel clock, and Lumiere helped him prepare, assuring

him that he looked handsome and elegant.

When he saw Belle in her ball gown, the Beast bowed

in admiration. At dinner he behaved like a perfect

gentleman and when Mrs Potts began to sing a love song,

Belle and the Beast danced in the ballroom, happy in

each other's arms.

Watching from the doorway, the servants were full of

joy. But they could not have guessed that the Beast's love

for Belle would send her away. "You are free to go," he told her. He could not bear to keep her prisoner.

Belle left to visit her father, who was ill. One of the villagers wanted to marry Belle but she knew she loved the Beast, and refused. An angry mob went to attack the Beast's castle.

The Beast was missing Belle so much

that he let them come in. Belle realised that she belonged with the Beast and tried to stop the mob. But she was too late. The Beast lay wounded and dying.

"At least I got to see you one last time," he said, gazing into her eyes.

"Don't die!" she cried. "I love you."

Suddenly, beams of light rained down from the sky.

The Beast returned to his human form. In amazement, Belle stared at the handsome prince in front of her.

"Belle, it's me," he assured her.

Looking deep into his eyes, she saw her friend's gentleness and love.

"It is you!" she cried. She kissed him joyfully. Then Mrs Potts and all the other servants became human once more. The happy couple celebrated with a fantastic ball in their shining castle. As they danced, all eyes basked in the timeless love of Beauty and the Beast.

DISNEY's

MULAN

FRIENDLY ADVICE

Long ago, far beyond the Great Wall of China, a young girl, Mulan, cut her hair and dressed as a man to take her elderly father's place in the war against the fierce Huns. Mushu, a tiny dragon, had been told by the

Ancestors to ask the Great Stone Dragon to act as Mulan's Guardian and adviser but Mushu decided he could do the job himself. "Punch people in the arm and call them names. That's what soldiers like," he advised.

Every time Mushu gave her advice, Mulan caused

more trouble. Soon all of the new recruits were fighting. The camp was in total chaos when Captain Shang arrived.

"My name is . . . uh . . . Ping," Mulan told Shang, as she awkwardly tried to sound like a man.

Shang had recently been promoted, and was wary of possible troublemakers.

Shang was a strong and skilful leader, and although Mulan

felt clumsy and inadequate, she worked hard and used her mind to finally win his respect. All of the soldiers admired Ping's determination and they were inspired by her actions. Still, not even her best friends,

Chien-Po, Ling and Yao, knew that "Ping" was a woman.

Shang led his troops swiftly to join the Imperial Army. Mulan and her friends sang songs. Sadly, their good cheer came to a halt when they discovered that the army and the

village lay in ruins. Shang was especially upset when he realised that his father, the General, had been killed in battle. As Mulan tried to comfort him, the Huns returned.

Proving to be a great and courageous soldier, Mulan caused an avalanche that buried the enemy. She was wounded, but saw that Shang was being buried in the snow and managed to pull him out just in time.

As Chien-Po and the others helped them to safety,
Shang looked at Mulan with admiration. "You saved my
life. From now on you have my trust," Shang said,
thanking her. Mulan's smile soon turned to pain, and as

her wound was
treated, they all
learned the truth
about "Ping."

At this time in
China, Mulan's
deception was
punishable by death,

but Shang spared her. "A life for a life," he declared. She could no longer serve in the army however.

Dejected, Mulan watched the troops march away, leaving her alone with Mushu. With a heavy heart Mulan confided in her friend, "I just wanted to do things properly, so that when I looked in the mirror I would see someone worthwhile. But I was wrong. I see nothing."

Trying to make her feel better, Mushu confessed that he had set out to make Mulan a hero so that he could impress the Ancestors. "At least you risked your life to help people you love. I risked your life to help myself," he told her. Mulan embraced the little dragon. How could

she be angry with such a friend?

This quiet moment was shattered as Mulan realised that a few of the Huns had

survived the avalanche.
Racing to the Imperial
City to warn Shang,
Mulan arrived moments
before the Emperor was
taken prisoner.

Chien-Po, Ling and
Yao tried unsuccessfully
to break down the palace
door. "I have an idea!"
Mulan called. Eager for
the help of their quick-

thinking friend, they let Mulan dress them as women. Together they scaled the wall and attacked the unsuspecting Huns. Realising that he could trust her, Shang soon

followed her lead. They rescued the Emperor, but Shan Yu, the Hun leader, angrily attacked Shang. To protect him, Mulan revealed herself as the soldier who had defeated Shan Yu at the mountain.

Shan Yu began to chase her ferociously. The girl and the dragon put their heads together and hatched a plan. Leading Shan Yu to the palace roof, Mulan grabbed his sword and pinned his cloak to the roof just as Mushu

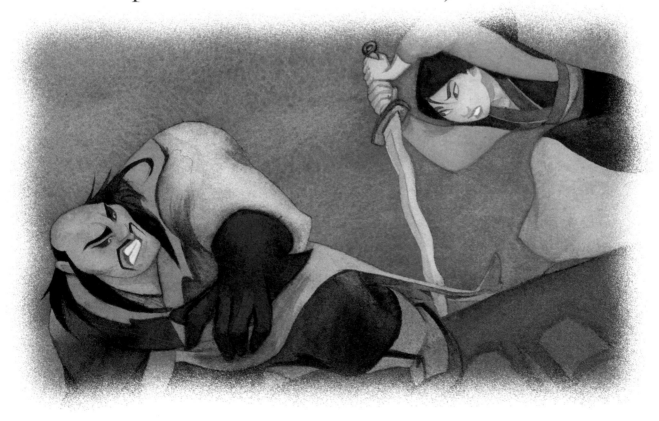

shot a rocket towards him. Shan Yu was blasted into a tower of fireworks.

Mulan was happy to leave for home. She realised that she was special enough as herself, and that she had friends she could count on. She presented the Emperor's sword to her father, and he welcomed her back. Shang followed her, realising, with the Emperor's help, that his feelings for Mulan had grown. She was much more than a good fighter. Finally, Mulan's heart

was full.

As for Mushu, the joyful little dragon was a hero. He celebrated with the happy Ancestors.

Disney's

DUMBO

If Not for Friends . . .

Dumbo the elephant felt all alone at the circus. His mother had been locked away for trumpeting at a child who had laughed at Dumbo's enormous ears. The other elephants blamed Dumbo for his mother's imprisonment. They laughed at his big ears too and turned

their backs on him when he most needed friendship and understanding.

In disbelief, a friendly mouse named Timothy

listened to the mean-spirited gossip of the large elephants.

Knowing that they would be terrified of a little mouse like

him, he decided to give them the fright of their life. After

all, someone had to stick up for little Dumbo. What was

wrong with having big ears anyway? thought Timothy.

As far as he was
concerned, Dumbo
was a cute baby
elephant.

So Timothy
waved his arms and
stuck out his

tongue. The elephants shrieked in fear, climbing poles to get away from the small mouse. "Pick on someone your own size!" yelled Timothy.

He chuckled at their silliness. "Imagine, being afraid of a small mouse," he laughed. "Wait till I tell little Dumbo." But Dumbo was scared of Timothy, too. He hid himself in

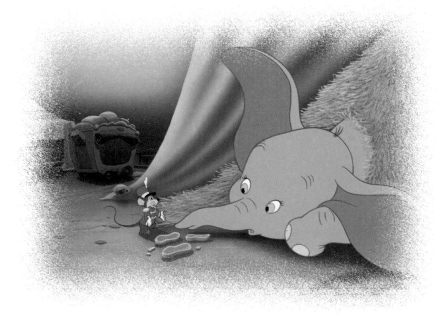

a bale of hay and would not come out even for a peanut.

"I'm your friend," Timothy

assured him. He told Dumbo that his ears were special.

Then he promised to help him get his mother set free if

the little elephant would come out. Hesitantly, Dumbo

finally looked out at his new protector. "We'll make you a

star of the circus," said

Timothy confidently.

He came up with a

cunning plan. Sneaking

into the ringmaster's

tent that night, the

mouse whispered his

great idea into the

sleeping man's ear. Thinking the idea had come to him in a dream, the ringmaster announced his amazing new act: Dumbo, the baby elephant, leaping from a springboard to the top of an amazing pyramid of bigger elephants!

Dumbo was nervous, and as he ran towards the

springboard, he tripped over his ears and fell, not only knocking over the enormous pyramid of elephants, but also causing the tent to collapse.

After that, to make matters worse, the ringmaster made Dumbo a clown. The poor little fellow didn't trust the other clowns to keep him safe. The ringmaster dressed Dumbo up as a baby and forced him to jump from a burning building.

Dumbo had never been so scared and humiliated! When the show was over, the

little elephant was inconsolable.

Timothy tried to comfort his friend. He offered peanuts as he washed the clown paint off with warm, soapy water. Still, Dumbo did not stop crying. Timothy knew that the only one who could help Dumbo now was his mother. So Timothy took him to see her.

Even though only her trunk could hug him, Dumbo basked in his mother's love. Although he was sad to go back to his tent without her, Dumbo was thankful for Timothy's help.

The next morning, after some strange and restless dreams, the mouse and the elephant awoke high up in a tree! Dumbo was so surprised that he lost his balance. Some crows laughed as the friends fell out of the tree into a pond.

"Don't listen to those crows," Timothy told Dumbo, but the elephant was already walking away, head down. Everyone was always laughing at him, him and his big

ears. Only Timothy believed they would do great things.

"That's it,

Dumbo!" cried his friend. Timothy had been trying to

work out how they had got up into that tree, when

suddenly he realised how special Dumbo's ears really

were. The perfect wings! "You can fly!" cheered Timothy.

This news made the crows fall over laughing. "Have

you ever seen an

elephant fly?" they

jeered.

Defending his

friend, Timothy

yelled at the crows

for being so

insensitive. "How would you like to be taken away from your mother when you were just a baby and then be sent out into a cold, cruel, heartless world?" he ranted.

The crows apologised. They really hadn't meant any harm.

"What he needs is this magic feather," offered one crow.

Timothy showed his friend: "Look, Dumbo, you can fly!"

Holding the feather in his trunk, Dumbo closed his eyes and flapped his ears. He wanted so much to believe Timothy! He was flying!

When he opened his eyes again the little elephant was

overjoyed. He held the feather tightly, flying through the sky like a bird. Timothy cheered from his seat on Dumbo's hat while the crows praised the elephant's talent.

That night Timothy's prediction of stardom came true.

At the circus, Dumbo stood at the top of the burning building. He didn't feel frightened – now he had the magic feather, he knew he could fly down safely. But just as he leaped into the air, he dropped the feather and panicked. As Dumbo began to fall, Timothy cried "Flap your ears! You can fly!" Dumbo flapped his ears and FLEW, astonishing everyone who had once made

fun of the elephant's big ears.

Finally, the ringmaster was so pleased that he ordered the release of Dumbo's mother and the pair were reunited! With love and pride, Timothy agreed to become manager of the world's only flying elephant!

Disney's

The Fox and the Hound

FRIENDS FOREVER

Tod was a fox and Copper was a hound. They played hide-and-seek, they swam in the water and they wrestled and ran together. Since they were unaware that a fox and a hound were not supposed to play together, a

friendship
developed. Each
morning they
looked forward to
meeting in the
woods for another
day of carefree fun.

"We'll always be
friends, won't we,
Copper?" Tod
asked one day as they splashed in the pond.

Copper agreed. They were best friends. Neither could

think of a reason why that should change as they chased

each other in the afternoon light.

Then one morning, Tod was disappointed when

Copper did not come to play. Amos, the puppy's master,

had decided that it was

time for Copper to learn

to hunt, like his old dog,

Chief. Copper loved

Chief like a father. He

was eager to impress

him and soon learned

how to track the scents

of many animals, including foxes.

While Copper was away, Tod was lonely. Mrs Tweed, who had cared for Tod since he was orphaned as a cub, kept him company during the long winter. Still, the growing fox missed his friends. He missed Big Mama, the owl, with her exciting stories and wise advice. He missed the silly antics of his bird friends, Dinky and Boomer, as they tried unsuccessfully to capture a caterpillar. Most of all, he missed playing with his friend Copper.

When spring finally came, he raced outside, overjoyed to be outdoors. As he talked excitedly to Big Mama, Dinky and Boomer, he heard Amos Slade's truck coming

down the road. Copper was home!

His friends tried to warn Tod that Copper would be different now that he was a hunting dog, but Tod refused to believe that Copper would ever become his enemy. "Copper's my friend!" he insisted.

That night, while Chief and Amos slept, Tod paid a visit to his old pal. He was surprised when Copper said, "We can't play together any more." As the fox tried to convince his friend to reconsider, Chief woke up and raced after Tod.

When Amos
ordered Copper to help
track the fox, the
hound led the hunter
and Chief in the wrong
direction on purpose.
"I don't want to see

you get hurt," Copper whispered to the scared fox. "Run
that way." Tod obeyed happily, realising that their
friendship wasn't over yet.

When the fox returned home, Mrs Tweed was very
anxious. She wanted to keep Tod safe and happy, but knew

that she could no longer protect him from Amos. Sadly, she hugged the fox, removed his collar, and left him in a wildlife sanctuary where she thought he would be safe.

The first night was long and difficult. Tod was scared and confused. He missed his warm home and his friends.

Beginning to despair, he caught sight of the most beautiful creature he had ever seen! It was Vixey, whom Big Mama had called upon to help the lonely fox. She batted her lovely eyelashes with a sweet "Hello," and Tod was in love.

Happily, the two foxes roamed the wilderness together. Vixey soon taught Tod how to fish and how to cope in his new forest home. Big Mama, Dinky and Boomer even came to

visit, and Tod knew that everything would be all right.

That evening, as he and Vixey were returning to their den, Tod spied a shiny object in the leaves. *Snap! Snap!*

Snap! went the traps that Amos had set.

Although hunting wasn't allowed in the sanctuary, Amos and Copper were after Tod. They blamed him for injuries that Chief had suffered when the hounds had last chased Tod.

With speed and courage, Tod and Vixey managed to get away from Amos and Copper when, suddenly, a grizzly bear leaped out and attacked the hunters. Tod

couldn't let his old friend come to harm, so he risked his

own life to lead the bear to a waterfall. As Tod climbed on

to the bank breathlessly, Amos pointed his rifle at the fox.

"If he wants to kill you, he'll have to shoot me first,"

said Copper as he stepped in front of his old friend.

Copper knew that Tod had risked his own life to save

him and his master and he finally realised how important

friendship was. A true friend, like Tod, would be a

friend forever.

In peace and contentment, Tod and Vixey remained together, their love blossoming in the freedom of their forest home. Occasionally Tod would look upon Copper from a cliff above the valley, knowing that even time, distance and the laws of nature could not break the bond between them.

Disney · PIXAR

a bug's life

FOR THE LOVE OF A PRINCESS

It was harvest time on Ant Island and all the ants were busy picking grain. Suddenly a young ant named Flik rushed over to Princess Atta, the ant in charge, bringing his latest invention. But Atta wasn't impressed – Flik's inventions never worked. "Just pick grain like everyone else," she sighed.

But Atta's younger sister Princess Dot believed in

Flik, even when his inventions caused trouble. After all, he was a clever ant, and a good listener. Flik was always kind to Dot and cheered her up when she felt sad about being so small.

A gang of grasshoppers was terrorising the ant colony, and Flik decided to go to the city to search for rough bugs that could fight the grasshoppers. The other ants did not think that Flik would make it back alive. But Princess Dot believed in him. She waved confidently to her friend as he sailed away on a dandelion seed.

Soon Flik returned. "You did it!" Dot cheered, but Princess Atta was worried. Could the assortment of bugs he had with him really conquer the grasshoppers? No one

knew that Flik had, in fact, brought back a troupe of circus performers who thought that Flik wanted them to put on a show!

Atta was won over when the strange group bravely rescued Dot from the path of a hungry bird. "Hooray!"

shouted the ants. Their applause stunned the circus bugs.

No one had ever appreciated them before. They were

filled with pride as the colony treated them like heroes. A

group of young ants, called the Blueberry scouts, asked

for autographs. The circus troupe decided to stay a while,

but they made it clear to Flik that they were not fighters.

He assured them that with his new plan, they would not
have to fight. "Your rescue gave me an idea," he said.
"Let's build a mechanical bird to frighten the
grasshoppers and their leader, Hopper."

After Dot's rescue, Princess Atta pulled Flik aside. "I
want to apologise," she told him, explaining her doubts

about the warriors. "I was afraid of making a mistake. No one believes that I'll be a good queen. It's as if they're all waiting for me to fail." Flik understood.

Princess Atta knew that Flik did understand, and she felt guilty for not believing in him. She was proud to be a part of Flik's new plan, and she directed the colony to follow his orders as they all built a bird to chase Hopper

and his bully followers away for good.

When the bird was finished, Flik told the circus bugs

they could leave, but they had changed their minds. They

believed in Flik. "I don't want to go," stated Dim, the giant blue bug, and the others agreed.

At that moment, P.T. Flea, the circus owner, came looking for his circus bugs. He told the ants that they had put their faith in circus performers, not warriors. Atta couldn't believe that Flik had lied to her! She had trusted him! Now she

angrily sent him away with his circus pals.

"It's okay," the circus bugs comforted the forlorn Flik.

"Being a circus performer's not such a bad life."

But Flik was too unhappy to be cheered up. When Dot

caught up with them, Flik was still feeling worthless. She

and the circus bugs believed

that his plan would work if

only they could convince

Flik to trust in himself.

Dot knew how. She

reminded him how he had

encouraged her when she felt small and helpless. Nodding gratefully to Dot, Flik returned to Ant Island with her and the circus bugs.

That evening, as the grasshoppers feasted on the ants' grain, a circus bug parade rumbled into sight. "We are here to entertain you," they announced. The grasshoppers

were busy watching the circus act and didn't see Flik

climbing into the bird machine. When the grasshoppers

saw the 'bird' flying towards them, they ran for cover.

But then the bird burst into flames and Hopper saw Flik

climb out of it. He was angrier than ever.

When Hopper took Flik hostage, Princess Atta knew she was his only chance. She realised that he had always put the colony's interests first. Risking her own life, she

flew after them, grabbing Flik away from the grasshopper.

Flik advised Princess Atta to fly towards a bird's nest. She

trusted his wise instinct, and Hopper became lunch for

three hungry hatchling chicks. At last, the ants were free!

Happily, Atta and Flik returned to Ant Island. Flik

was proud to see Atta crowned Queen, and she happily appointed him the colony's official inventor. Thanks to Flik's courage, Hopper and his gang would never bother the ants again.

WALT DISNEY'S

Lady and the TRAMP

OPPOSITES ATTRACT

Lady was a pretty cocker spaniel and Tramp was a scruffy but handsome mongrel. One night, Tramp led Lady to an Italian restaurant where they ate the best spaghetti in town. The two dogs didn't realise that they

were eating the same strand of spaghetti until their noses met. Bashfully, Lady looked away. What a romantic night, they both thought as they walked around town with their stomachs full and the stars smiling down on the quiet streets.

With unspoken commitment they placed their paws side by side in wet cement, gazing at each other lovingly. Then Tramp guided

Lady through a peaceful park and they fell asleep. When Lady awoke at dawn she was happy, but startled to realise that she had been away from home for so long.

Tramp was surprised that Lady wanted to return to her fenced garden. "Open your eyes to what a dog's life can really be," he told her as they gazed at a beautiful view of the country. "Who knows what wonderful experiences two dogs can have, and it's all ours for the taking."

Lady smiled. "It sounds wonderful," she agreed. "But who'll watch over the new baby?"

Tramp realised that Lady was very loyal to her human

family. Jim Dear and Darling were very kind, giving her the best food, a warm home and lots of love. "With Lady here I think life is quite complete," Jim Dear had once said, and now that the baby had been born their lives were even more full. Lady felt needed in a way that she had never known before. She was anxious to get home in

order to protect the little one who had become very dear to her heart.

However, when she returned, Jim Dear and Darling were away visiting friends. Aunt Sarah, angry at Lady for running away, chained the poor dog to her kennel.

Misunderstood by the old woman, Lady was treated harshly, but thankfully Aunt Sarah did not attempt to put a muzzle on her.

With a heavy heart Lady resigned herself to a cold and lonely night, but no sooner had she settled down than she was startled awake. A large rat was sneaking into the garden!

Yanked roughly by her chain when she tried to give chase,

Lady watched helplessly as the rat scurried through an

open window to

the baby's room.

Fearfully, she

barked with all

her might.

"What's

wrong?" called

Tramp, running to

help. When Lady

explained, he

hurried to protect the baby and fought with the vicious rat until the creature was dead. Lady, who had tugged herself free, stood proudly by his side as Aunt Sarah entered to check on the crying baby.

"Merciful heavens!" Aunt Sarah exclaimed when she saw the cot overturned and the room in disarray. Not

seeing the rat, she blamed the two dogs and called the

dogcatcher to take Tramp away. Lady barked desperately.

Luckily, Jim Dear and Darling soon arrived home.

"She's trying to tell us something," Jim Dear insisted.

Quickly, Lady led them to the rat.

Overhearing the humans, Lady's friends Jock and

Trusty realised what had happened. "We've got to stop

the dogcatcher!" declared Trusty, chasing down the road.

Jock followed and they soon managed to track Tramp

down. However, when they attempted to make the

dogcatcher stop, the cart suddenly veered out of control.

It turned on its side, toppling onto poor old Trusty. Jock

was inconsolable until he discovered Trusty had only broken a leg.

Just then, Jim Dear and Darling arrived with Lady.

Jim Dear realised that Tramp had rescued the baby and invited him to live with them. Tramp found that some humans could be trusted after all. Living in a fenced garden wasn't so bad, thought Tramp as he proudly

showed Jock and Trusty his new collar and name tag.

That Christmas, as well as their human family, Lady and

Tramp had puppies of their own to watch over.

Disney's
The Rescuers

Small Mice, Big Hearts

One night, a nasty woman came and kidnapped Penny from the orphanage where she lived. "You're going to find diamonds for me in Devil's Bayou!" she told her. "Don't worry, Penny," Rufus the old cat said,

as Medusa dragged the child away. Rufus was sure that a

mother and father were looking for a girl just like Penny,

and would find her

in Devil's Bayou.

Medusa kept the

child prisoner on

an old boat in the

swamp. Penny tried

to escape, but

Medusa's pet

crocodiles found

her and brought

her back to the creepy riverboat.

Meanwhile, at the Rescue Aid Society, a message in a bottle had been found – from Penny. The chairman said, "Someone needs our help right now. Who will go to the rescue?"

The beautiful Miss Bianca had volunteered straight away, and when she chose Bernard the caretaker to be her assistant, he couldn't have been prouder.

"The Rescue Aid Society is depending on us," Bianca reminded her friend. Bernard nodded. He was only a caretaker for the Society, but no mouse was more loyal.

"Don't worry, Teddy. We'll be all right!" Penny sobbed. As Penny prayed for help, the rescuers were climbing

through her window. "Penny," Bianca called softly. As the child raised her tear-stained face, the mice explained that they had found her message and had come to rescue her.

The mice told Penny that they'd had many adventures on the way. So far they had been nearly drowned, chased by crocodiles and shot at by Medusa. But with the aid of

a map, they'd found her at last.

Penny's eyes lit up. She twirled Teddy in the air excitedly. Then she stopped short. "Didn't you bring anyone big with you? Such as the police?"

Bernard shook his head. "But if the three of us work together, things will turn out all right," he said.

Together they came up with a plan. First Bernard sent for help from their friends who lived nearby. Penny showed them an old lift that would make a good cage for the crocodiles. They could light fireworks to distract

Medusa and escape on the swamp boat. "This is so exciting!" Bianca declared, hugging the bashful Bernard. Even Penny laughed for the first time in ages.

However, their fun did not last long. Medusa suddenly arrived and Bernard and Bianca quickly hid in Penny's pocket. "You're going to look in the cave for the Devil's Eye diamond!" shrieked Medusa.

"Teddy doesn't like

it down there!" pleaded the little girl, as Medusa lowered her into the dark cave in a bucket, but Medusa didn't care. She grabbed the teddy bear. "You'll find that diamond or you'll never see your precious Teddy again!"

Penny was so frightened she obeyed. The cave was spooky but at least Bernard and Bianca were there to help her this time. Suddenly the ground shook and they looked towards a gaping hole where water hissed and gurgled dangerously. "If I were a pirate that's just where I'd hide the Devil's Eye," said Bernard.

Although it was dangerous to get to the other side, the mice helped each other across the hole. Sure enough, the diamond was in there, hidden inside a skull! Bianca and Bernard tried to

pull it free, but the diamond was too big. "It's stuck tight!" Penny yelled to Medusa. The tide was coming in fast, but Medusa would not pull her to safety. "You'll bring me that diamond or you'll never see daylight again!" she roared.

Bravely, Penny crossed the hole and prised the skull open just as the water rushed in. Caught in a whirlpool, Bernard and Bianca cried for help. As Penny risked her life

to save her friends, a wave tossed them into the bucket.

"Give me back my Teddy!" cried Penny, as Medusa

snatched the diamond out of reach of her fat friend,

Snoops. Hiding the diamond in the bears' stuffing,

Medusa held Penny at bay with her gun. Luckily, Bernard and Bianca thought quickly. They tied a wire across the doorway, causing Medusa to trip.

As Penny snatched Teddy, the Rescuers ran after her

and climbed aboard the swamp boat. "We did it!" cheered

Bernard when they were safe.

When she got back to the orphanage, Penny found to

her delight that she had been adopted. The next day,

Bernard, Bianca and the chairman of the Rescue Aid

Society watched Penny on television. Penny stood with Teddy and her new parents. "Two little mice rescued me," she told the world. She'd never forget her brave friends!

Walt Disney's Bambi

SMITTEN

As Prince Bambi learned to walk, an outspoken young rabbit named Thumper became his cheerful guide in the forest. Clumsily, Bambi stumbled after Thumper and his brothers and sisters. "He's a little wobbly, isn't he?" asked Thumper, and the bunnies all giggled as the little prince got used to his thin, young legs.

As they explored, Bambi stopped to

look at some beautifully coloured birds. "Say *bird*," Thumper prompted. "Burr . . ." tried the little fawn.

"Bir-duh!" Thumper corrected. Soon Bambi was saying his first word as the bunnies happily cheered him on.

Butterfly and then *flower* were the next words Bambi learned. Thumper showed him how to smell the fragrant

blooms, but when Bambi leaned into the flowers he touched a small black nose. "Flower!" the fawn pronounced

proudly. Thumper rolled over laughing as he saw a skunk lift his head from the blossoms. "He's not a flower," Thumper began to explain. "He's a little . . ."

"That's all right," interrupted the bashful skunk. "He can call me Flower if he wants to." Happy with his new name, Flower held a special place in his heart for the young prince.

Soon after, while playing in the meadow, the little deer captured another heart. When he was looking at his reflection in the water, the pretty face of a female fawn, Faline, appeared beside his own. In shock, Bambi jumped backwards. Suddenly he was shy as he looked into the other

fawn's big blue eyes.

Faline laughed heartily at Bambi's nervousness. Bounding towards him, she caused him to stumble through some reeds and land with a splash in the creek. Mischievously, the doe teased her playmate by leaning through the reeds to kiss him, then running around to lick his other cheek.

Bambi was not nearly as amused as his tormentor.

"You!" he yelled, pouncing at Faline. She giggled and ran and he chased her through the meadow, his anger changing quickly to enjoyment. It was fun to have another deer to play with.

Quickly, the seasons changed. Bambi woke one morning and he was amazed to see the world covered in white. "It's snow," his mother explained. "Winter has come."

Indeed it had! Bambi and Thumper revelled in the winter wonderland. Thumper even tried to teach his friend to ice skate, but hooves and long, thin legs are not meant for slippery surfaces. Thumper patiently pushed,

pulled and prodded to keep Bambi upright. Flower,

however, did not share in their merriment. "All of us

flowers sleep in the winter," he informed the others.

As the seasons passed, Bambi and his friends became

handsome young males. Friend Owl warned them that

they would soon find themselves "smitten" – falling in love.

"It won't happen to me!" each of the three friends declared. Haughtily, they walked away.

Then, without warning, Flower felt his heart pumping.

Two of the prettiest blue eyes he had ever seen were staring at him through a garden of daisies. As the female skunk kissed him, Flower turned red all over. Smiling, he followed her through the blossoms, turning only once to

give Bambi and Thumper a helpless shrug. "Smitten!" cried Thumper. He listened to the happy giggles as Flower bounded after the lovely female skunk. In disbelief, he and Bambi continued down the path.

Suddenly, Thumper stopped in his tracks! He turned to look at a gorgeous bunny fluffing the fur on her cheeks. With a flutter of long eyelashes and a kiss, Thumper's foot began thumping wildly. Owl was right.

He had fallen in love. Now Bambi was alone. As he stopped for a drink at the creek, he saw Faline. She had grown into a beautiful doe. Bambi was startled at her reflection and backed into a blossoming tree, catching his antlers in the branches. "Hello, Bambi." She laughed gently. "Remember me?"

This time she wasn't teasing as she leaned to kiss him, and he wasn't rubbing the kiss away as he had when they were fawns. Instead, his eyes grew big and round. He bounded after Faline as if in a dream filled with clouds.

As they pranced through the meadow, Bambi was so happy he felt as if he was flying.

Deciding to spend their lives together, Bambi and Faline soon became proud parents of a pair of fawns. All of the animals in the forest came to gaze at Bambi's children. Thumper brought his large family. Even Flower had a little baby skunk to hurry along. How happy Bambi was to have everyone he loved

share his joy!

Snow White and the Seven Dwarfs

FRIENDS TO COUNT ON

Once there lived a princess named Snow White. Her wicked stepmother, the Queen, was so jealous of Snow White's beauty that she ordered her huntsman to take the girl into the forest and kill her. But the man let

her run away
instead. As night
fell, Snow White
became very afraid!

The woodland
animals came to gaze
at the lovely princess
and watched over her all night.

In the morning, as the birds began to sing she joined
them. Singing always made her feel better. She asked the
animals if they knew where she might stay. They led Snow
White to a clearing where she noticed a little cottage.

Snow White entered and found there was no one home. The room was dirty with dishes piled high in the sink and clothes tossed about. As she counted the adorable little chairs at the table, Snow White thought seven untidy children must live in this cottage. Perhaps they have no mother, she thought sadly. Snow

White decided to surprise them by cleaning and making

dinner, and sang a cheerful song as she worked. The

squirrels, chipmunks, deer, raccoons and birds helped her

dust, wash and

sweep. Snow

White put soup

on to cook, then

climbed upstairs

where she

discovered seven

little beds. Names

were carved into

each one: Doc, Happy, Sneezy, Dopey, Grumpy, Bashful and Sleepy. What strange names for children, she thought, but the beds looked wonderfully inviting and she was awfully tired. As she lay across three of the small

mattresses, the birds covered her tenderly with a blanket, and Snow White fell fast asleep.

Soon seven dwarfs came home. "The whole house is clean!"

Doc

exclaimed.

Nervously

they tiptoed

upstairs.

Seeing a large

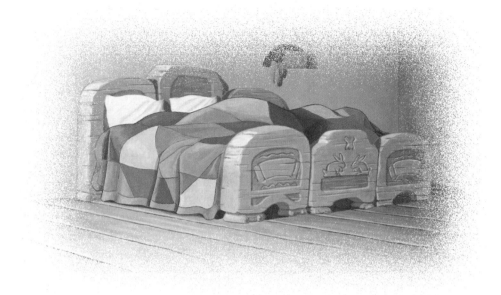

form under the sheets, they assumed it was a monster and

got ready to attack as Snow White began to stir. They

stared at the beautiful girl in surprise. "An angel,"

whispered Bashful, but Grumpy thought differently. "All

females are poison!" he insisted.

The nervous dwarfs hid behind the bed. The Princess

was startled as they peeked at her over the foot of the bed. "Oh, you're little men!" she cried happily. Smiling, she guessed their names and explained how she had been sent away by her stepmother, the Queen. "She tried to kill me," Snow White told them, but Grumpy was unsympathetic.

"Send her away!" he yelled, nervous about the evil queen's black magic.

"She won't find me here," the Princess promised, "and I'll wash, and keep house and cook . . ."

The dwarfs thought of the food that Snow White could cook. "She can stay!" they agreed. They followed her downstairs as she went to check the soup.

"Wash your hands or you won't get a bite to eat!" said Snow White as she checked their dirty hands. Although the dwarfs dreaded soap and water, they wanted to make the Princess happy.

After dinner they played music and danced. Even Grumpy played the pipe organ. Never had they had so much fun or laughed so hard!

"Now you do something," they urged Snow White. She began to tell them a story about a princess who fell in love. "Was it you?" they asked, and she nodded, remembering the charming prince who had appeared as she was

singing at a wishing well.

Startled, Snow White had run into the castle, but when the Prince serenaded her, she looked out onto the balcony. "He was so romantic," she told her new friends. She had sent him a kiss on the wings of a dove.

Sighing dreamily, the dwarfs gave Snow White their cosy beds for the night. Even Grumpy was happy that she had stayed.

"I'm warning you – don't let anyone or anything in the house!" he said the next morning as he left for work.

"Why, Grumpy, you do care!" Snow White smiled as Grumpy stomped away. Then she kissed Dopey tenderly and sent him on his way.

Forgetting Grumpy's warning, Snow White allowed a poor old woman into the house that afternoon. The old woman offered her an apple, and not suspecting that it

was the Queen in disguise, the poor girl took one bite of the poisoned apple and fell to the floor.

The dwarfs and forest animals grieved for their beloved princess until the day a prince appeared, having heard the story of a lovely girl, lying in a glass coffin.

Recognising her as the princess he'd been searching for, he kissed her.

Slowly, Snow White awakened. The happy prince

lifted her in his arms as the dwarfs and animals rejoiced around them. Cheerfully giving each of her friends a good-bye kiss, Snow White turned to her true love. As the birds sang, the happy couple walked towards a golden castle, where they lived happily ever after.

DISNEY'S

Aladdin

THE PRINCESS
WHO DIDN'T WANT TO MARRY

Long ago, there lived the lovely Princess Jasmine. One day, her father the Sultan said, "The law says you must be married to a prince by your next birthday."

Jasmine thought the law was unfair. She wanted to marry for love. Her father wanted her to marry Prince

Achmed but Jasmine thought he was selfish. She asked her pet tiger, Rajah, to chase him away. He returned with a piece of Prince Achmed's trousers in his mouth.

Rajah and Jasmine were glad to be rid of her unwanted suitor.

Jasmine wished that she wasn't a princess at all. She felt as trapped as the caged doves. That night she disguised herself, planning to escape.

As she began to climb over the palace wall, Rajah tugged on her dress. He was sad to see Jasmine leave, but knew what was best for her. "I can't stay here and have my life lived for me," she explained sorrowfully.

In the market place, life was busy and exciting. Jasmine felt sorry for a

poor child and handed him an apple from a stall. However,

when she was unable to pay, the stallholder grabbed her

angrily. Just then, a handsome stranger came to her rescue.

Running fast, they escaped to his rooftop home.

Jasmine was thrilled with the thought of such freedom. This young man had no one to tell him what he could or couldn't do. As she was imagining his carefree life, the man looked longingly towards the palace. It would be

wonderful to live there, he thought, without having to worry about where to find his next meal.

"Sometimes I just feel so trapped," they both expressed at the same time.

Surprised, they looked at each other. Feeling a deep bond with this handsome stranger, Jasmine leaned to kiss

him, when
suddenly
guards burst
upon them.
There was
nowhere to
escape.

"Do you
trust me?" asked the young man, holding out his hand to
her. She looked into his brown eyes and placed her
fingers in his grip.

Quickly, they jumped off the tall building, their fall

broken by a pile of hay. "I've got you this time, Street Rat!" yelled another guard, grabbing hold of the young man.

Jasmine revealed herself as a princess but they still arrested her friend. "My orders come from Jafar, the Sultan's chief advisor," the guard told her.

Back at the palace, Jasmine confronted Jafar. The evil man cruelly deceived her into thinking that her handsome stranger was dead. "Oh, Rajah," she wept, as the tiger tried to comfort her.

Many days later, on the streets of Agrabah, there was a magnificent parade. Princess Jasmine, still grieving, watched from her balcony. Trumpets were blaring, animals were doing tricks, fireworks blasted, but most impressive was a prince called Ali, sitting on top of an enormous elephant, throwing gold coins into the crowd. Jasmine shook her head in disgust. Did he think he could buy her hand in marriage?

With anger, she yelled at the prince, "I am not a prize to be won!" But Prince Ali would not give up. That evening he appeared on her balcony. Rajah growled protectively and was about to chase him away but

Jasmine thought he looked familiar. She stepped closer and he showed her his magic carpet. "We could see the world,"

Prince Ali offered.

Jasmine hesitated until he leaned forward offering his hand. "Do you trust me?" he asked, and immediately Jasmine knew this was the same stranger she had met in the market place. Eagerly she climbed aboard and the carpet took them into the star-filled sky. Never had she seen such wonders! As they flew, she felt happier than she ever had before.

Unfortunately, Jafar soon discovered that the "prince" had a magic lamp. Aladdin had used a wish from a genie in the lamp to transform himself into Prince Ali.

Jafar revealed to Jasmine that the man she loved was Aladdin, a poor boy from Agrabah.

"Jasmine, I'm sorry I lied to you about being a prince," said

Aladdin in a humble voice. Jasmine held his hands. She didn't love him for being a prince. She loved Aladdin for himself.

Even the Sultan realised that Aladdin was worthy. When her father changed the law to allow his daughter to marry the man of her choice, Jasmine said, "I choose Aladdin."

As fireworks lit the sky, Aladdin and Jasmine shared a kiss on their magic carpet. Beneath them was a whole new world where they would live happily ever after.

DISNEY's

POCAHONTAS

LISTEN TO YOUR HEART

Ayoung Native American girl named Pocahontas looked into the wise face of her ancient friend, Grandmother Willow. Troubled by a dream about a spinning arrow, she wondered, "What is my path?"

Grandmother Willow told her there were spirits in the

earth, water and sky. "If you listen they will guide you."

Climbing to the top of a tree, Pocahontas felt the wind

around her and saw strange white clouds in the distance.

The clouds were sails of a ship that carried strangers from

England to the

land. Pocahontas

secretly watched

an adventurous

man exploring the

forest that

afternoon. She was

drawn towards him, following in his footsteps until suddenly he jumped out of the shadows. The two stared at each other for many moments. Captain John Smith had never seen a woman so beautiful and mysterious. He wanted to get closer, but his movement scared Pocahontas, who ran like a deer, away to the river where she kept her canoe.

"Wait," he called as he ran after her. "I'm not going to hurt you." Although he spoke a different language, she listened with her heart.

"I'm Pocahontas," she told him as she took his outstretched hand. Together they talked and bonded in a way that Pocahontas had never experienced before. They laughed at Meeko, a mischievous raccoon, who rummaged for biscuits in John's bag. Pocahontas quietened Flit, her hummingbird

friend, who flew in John's face, protecting her.

Pocahontas knew in her heart the goodness inside John

Smith, and realised she was safe.

Pocahontas began to sing, guiding him through the forest. "We are all connected to each other," she told him. She showed him the gentleness of a mother bear with her cubs. They listened to the wolves cry and watched eagles fly to the top of a sycamore tree. "How tall does a sycamore grow?" asked Pocahontas. "You'll never know if you cut it down."

As nature touched his soul, John Smith began to

realise that his people had much to learn. With

Pocahontas as his teacher, he could hear the voices in the

mountains and even see colours in the wind. This amazing

young woman was right. No one owned the land.

Understanding, he held her hands and gazed into her brown eyes.

Back at the village, Pocahontas' childhood friend Nakoma was worried about her. Fighting had broken out between the strangers and the villagers, yet when John Smith appeared in the cornfield Pocahontas made her promise not to tell anyone. Nakoma kept her silence but felt uncomfortable as she watched the

two figures disappear into the evening shadows.

Pocahontas led John to Grandmother Willow while

Meeko and Flit chased after their new playmate, Percy, a dog

from the settler's camp. The ancient eyes looked kindly into

John's blue ones. "He has a good soul," she told Pocahontas,

"and he's

handsome, too."

John Smith

laughed. "Oh, I

like her," he said.

Pocahontas was

very happy. When

John Smith left, Grandmother Willow suggested that

perhaps Pocahontas had found her path.

Nakoma disagreed. She pleaded with Pocahontas not

to see John Smith again, but her friend vanished into the

woods anyway. In fear, Nakoma sent a warrior to look for Pocahontas. When they returned, John Smith had been taken prisoner and Pocahontas fell to her knees with grief. "I'm sorry," said Nakoma, taking her hands. "I

thought I was doing the right thing."

In the prisoner's tepee, Pocahontas cried. "I'd rather die tomorrow than live a hundred years without knowing you," John Smith told her tenderly.

Pocahontas went to see Grandmother Willow. She wanted to do something, but how could one girl stop a war between two peoples? "I feel so lost," she told the tree spirit. Meeko's ears perked up. Quickly the little raccoon found a compass he had taken from John Smith's

bag. Perhap it would help Pocahontas find her way. Inside was a spinning arrow. "My dream!" exclaimed the young woman.

She knew what her path was as she courageously addressed the fighting villagers. Protecting John Smith with her own body she proved that love is stronger than hatred. Although peace ensued, John Smith had already been wounded.

Heavy-hearted, Pocahontas knew that he would have to return to London if he was to survive. "I'll always be with you," she told him, and she kissed him good-bye. As she watched his ship sail away, the wind touched them both once again.

THE
LION KING

FRIENDSHIP MEANS NO WORRIES

Simba carried a heavy burden for a young lion. Timon, a meerkat, and Pumbaa, a warthog, wanted to help their troubled new friend.

"You've got to put the past behind you," Timon advised him. "Repeat after me . . . Hakuna Matata!"

This was Timon and Pumbaa's philosophy. "It means no worries," they sang, and soon Simba decided to stay

with them. With Pumbaa and Timon as his playmates, Simba began to enjoy himself again. The trio feasted on bugs, swam in the river, sang songs, told jokes and slept

under the stars.

Life was good as long as Simba didn't think about painful memories – how his father Mufasa had died when Simba was a cub, and his uncle Scar saying that Simba was responsible. Scar had told him to run away and never return to the pride again.

One afternoon Simba's childhood playmate, Nala, came hunting. The lioness had no idea that her friend was

still alive. She was searching for food and had chosen Pumbaa as her target.

"Help, Simba! She's going to eat me!" cried the petrified warthog, who was stuck under a tree root.

Just in time, Simba jumped to the rescue. Only after Nala had pinned him to the ground did he recognise his old childhood friend.

"Nala!" he cried joyfully. Thrilled that Simba was alive, the lioness pranced around him in disbelief.

"This is Nala. She's my best friend," Simba said to Timon and Pumbaa. The two lions had been playmates when they were cubs. Even when Simba had led her to the dangerous elephant graveyard, Nala stuck by his side.

"I thought you were very brave," she had whispered as they were led home. Simba was glad to see her again.

"You don't know how much this will mean to everyone . . . what it means to me," Nala told him. "I've really missed you."

Simba nuzzled her. "I've missed you, too," he said, but he was still not ready to return to the pride with Nala.

Together the lions walked in the magic evening air. They chased each other through the grass and tumbled down a hill. As they landed softly, Nala kissed Simba. It was a wonderful tender moment and the two embraced.

"Why didn't you come back?" Nala eventually asked.

Simba had been waiting for this question and hung his head in shame. "No one needs me," he responded, but Nala disagreed. She told him that Scar had let the hyenas destroy the Pride Lands. "If you don't do something soon, everyone will starve," she told him. "You're our only hope."

Still, Simba was not ready to return. He walked guiltily

away. "You can't change the
past," he said to himself,
"and it's all my fault."

Close by, the wise baboon
Rafiki called out to him.
"You're Mufasa's boy," he
reminded Simba. Then he
led the lion to a pool of
water and told him to look
hard at his reflection. "He lives in you!" the baboon
told him.

Suddenly the clouds changed shape and Simba saw his

father. "Remember who you are," Mufasa said from the stars. "You are my son and the one true king."

Simba was afraid of what he knew he must do. Knocking some sense into his friend, Rafiki struck the lion with his stick. Simba was surprised.

"Why did you do that?"

"It doesn't matter. It's in the past," Rafiki told him.

"The past can hurt. You can either run from it or learn from it." As Rafiki swung his stick again, Simba ducked, avoiding the blow. Now that he understood the lesson, he was ready to return to the Pride Lands to challenge his uncle.

Sadly, he looked at the destruction Scar had caused. "If I don't fight for it, who will?" he wondered.

"I will," Nala answered, joining him proudly. Timon and Pumbaa had followed as well. "Simba, if it's important to you, we're beside you to the end," they told him.

The three followed Simba to Pride Rock. Everyone

fought in the battle, even old Rafiki. The lionesses chased

the hyenas away while Simba took care of Scar.

"I killed Mufasa," admitted his evil uncle. Anger surged through Simba: anger for the death of his father, anger for years of guilt, anger for the destruction of his home. Using a trick that Nala taught him, he flipped Scar over a cliff.

With a great roar, Simba finally claimed his rightful

place as king. The lionesses echoed his proclamation and

happily welcomed him home. As news of Simba's return

spread, animals once again roamed free. The land began to heal, and Simba and Nala started a family of their own.

DISNEY's
ROBIN HOOD

PRINCE OF OUTLAWS

Long ago in Sherwood Forest there lived two outlaws. Their names were Robin Hood and Little John. They were clever and fast and the best archers in the land. Prince John wanted them arrested and sent his soldiers after them, but they escaped. With their many

disguises and skills they stole his gold, jewels and once, even his royal robe.

The people of Nottingham thought of the outlaws as

heroes. When the Sheriff came to collect high taxes, Robin never failed to replenish the coins in the villagers' pockets.

Once the Sheriff even took a bunny's birthday money, leaving the large rabbit family penniless. When Robin Hood arrived, he gave little Skippy his bow and arrow and his hat to make up for the lost present. The bunnies were delighted and Mother Rabbit thanked him as he put a bag of gold in her hand.

"You risk so much to keep our hopes alive . . . bless you!" she called after him.

As Robin returned to his hideout, the beautiful Maid Marian was dreaming of her childhood sweetheart.

Staring at Robin Hood's "wanted" poster, she confided in her best friend, Lady Kluck. "Surely he must know how much I still love him," she sighed. With a smile Klucky assured her that they would be together soon.

Meanwhile, Robin was thinking of Maid Marian as well. "I love her, Johnny," he confessed. Little John was not surprised. "Just marry the girl," he advised, but Robin shook his head hopelessly. "What have I got to offer her?" he asked. "I'm an outlaw. What kind of a future is that?"

Just then Friar Tuck appeared. Overhearing the conversation, he became indignant. "Oh, for heaven's

sake, son!" he exclaimed. "You're not an outlaw. Someday you'll be called a great hero!"

Robin Hood and Little John laughed at the thought as Friar Tuck told them about an archery tournament. Maid Marian had promised a kiss to the winner. Robin's eyes gleamed. He could win the contest blindfolded!

In his greatest disguise yet, Robin entered the tournament with a wink at his love. "I wish you luck,"

Maid Marian told him. Then she whispered, "With all my heart."

Unknowingly, Robin had fallen right into a trap set by Prince John. As he won the contest, he was unmasked, arrested and sentenced to death.

"Please, no!" Maid Marian pleaded with Prince John. Confessing her love, she begged for Robin's life to be spared.

"Marian, my darling," Robin declared, "I love you

more than life itself."

The Prince refused to listen, but Little John would not let Robin down. With a knife pressed to Prince John's back, he forced the tyrant to release his friend. As the crowd cheered, Robin and Maid Marian embraced, but it wasn't long before the Sheriff of Nottingham worked out what was happening.

Quickly, Little John threw a sword towards Robin. While fending off the Sheriff's soldiers, Robin swept Maid Marian off her feet and asked her to marry him. "Darling, I thought you'd never ask," she answered happily. Even Lady Kluck joined the fight against the soldiers, and they all escaped to Sherwood Forest.

Together again, Maid Marian and Robin Hood kissed in the romance of a night filled with fireflies. Offering a ring made from flowers, Robin pledged his love to her and the two walked back to camp hand in hand.

Their merriment did not last long, however. Prince John was angry about being humiliated. Tripling the taxes, he ordered the Sheriff to arrest all who could not

pay. Unfortunately, the prison filled quickly. Even Friar Tuck was arrested.

Robin Hood and

Little John decided it was time to stage a jailbreak. They
knew the Sheriff would be on alert, but Robin was a
master of disguise. In no time, he had fooled the guards
and lulled the Sheriff to sleep, stealing his keys. As Little

John released the
prisoners, Robin
crept into Prince
John's bedroom and
removed every last
bag of gold.

Soon after, the
rightful king,

Richard, returned and sent Prince John and his servants to prison. As the friends all gathered to celebrate the joyful wedding of Robin Hood and Maid Marian, Nottingham was a happy, peaceful town once again.

THE LION KING II
SIMBA'S · PRIDE

LOVE WITHSTANDS ANYTHING

Kiara was warned never to go to the Outlands, but her father Simba the Lion King wouldn't tell her why. What could be so terrible? Kiara wondered curiously. As soon as her faithful guardians, Timon and

Pumbaa, were distracted by their favourite pastime of eating bugs, she crept towards the forbidden land.

There she met another lion cub named Kovu. The two cubs helped each other to cross a dangerous river full of crocodiles. Exhilarated by the adventure, Kiara exclaimed, "We make a good team!" With admiration she smiled at Kovu. "You were really brave," she told him.

He looked at her curiously. His mother, Zira, had always

taught him that Pride Landers couldn't be trusted, yet this lioness had saved him from the crocodile's teeth.

"Yes, you were pretty brave, too," Kovu admitted.

Happily, Kiara began to prance around him. She was laughing and wanted to play, but Kovu didn't understand.

He had never played tag. Just as Kiara began to make him smile and laugh, their parents arrived with bared teeth!

Kiara's father, Simba, was an enemy of Kovu's mother,

Zira. Because Zira was loyal to Scar, who had murdered

Simba's father, the Lion King had banished her to the

Outlands. Focused on revenge, Zira was raising Kovu to

hate. Her plan was to overthrow Simba and make her son the new King.

"Take your cub and get out!" Simba ordered. As they were separated, the cubs sadly whispered good-bye.

It was not until they were fully grown that the two saw each other again. Kiara was a beautiful young lioness out on her first hunt. She had made her father promise not to interfere, but Simba was protective of his only daughter. As usual, he sent Timon and Pumbaa to watch over her . . . from a distance.

When Kiara came upon Timon and Pumbaa during her chase, she felt betrayed and angry. Wanting to prove that she could manage on her own, she raced away to hunt in the Outlands. Unaware that Zira and the Outsiders were watching her every move, she fell into their trap easily.

Quickly Zira and her followers set the plains on fire in a circle around Kiara. The young lioness ran until she fell unconscious. It was then that Kovu appeared. Trained to avenge Scar, he rescued the Princess only to get closer to his goal of killing Simba. He was ready for anything . . . except falling in love.

"Thanks for saving me," Kiara said after Simba reluctantly allowed Kovu to return with her to Pride Rock. She was happy to have him back in her life and she unwittingly distracted Kovu from his mission. Leading him away from her father, Kiara asked him to impress her with his expertise in stalking.

As Kovu showed her how to pounce quietly, they ran into Timon and Pumbaa. The silly animals were trying to rid their feeding ground

of annoying birds. "Will you help us?" asked Timon. With

a roar, Kiara gave chase.

"Why are we doing this?" asked Kovu, puzzled. "For

fun!" answered Kiara. She showed Kovu the joy of

laughter, and he was exhilarated by the new experience.

Even after being chased by angry hippos he was happier than he had ever been. "What fun!" he shouted, smiling at Kiara. By accident, the two bumped noses bashfully. "You're okay, kid!" said Timon.

That night Kovu and Kiara lay on the grass looking at the stars. "Do you think Scar's up there?" Kovu asked tentatively. "He wasn't my father, but he is a part of me."

Kiara knew he was troubled and tried to comfort her friend, but he pulled away. Feeling confused, Kovu wasn't

sure if he should follow his mother's plan or follow his heart.

Nearby, the wise baboon, Rafiki, was watching. Leading the two lions to a place he called Upendi, Rafiki placed them in a boat. As Kovu watched Kiara during the wild ride, he gave in to his feelings for her. Kissing and laughing, Kiara guessed, "Upendi means love, doesn't it?"

Deciding not to follow in Scar's footsteps, Kovu made peace with Simba. When the Outsiders found out, they set a trap for Simba. He managed to escape but he believed Kovu was responsible for the trap, and exiled him.

Kiara was heartbroken. She knew that Kovu couldn't have been responsible for the trap, so she ran away and followed Kovu to a watering hole. "Hey, look! We are joined together," Kovu said, looking at their reflection together in the water. Now they knew their love could survive anything. Racing back to the Pride Lands, Kiara begged her father to make peace with the Outsiders. "We are one pride!" she declared.

With peace settling over Pride Rock once more, Simba accepted Kovu's love for Kiara. Together, they joined the King and Queen for a celebration of unity.

Disney's

Oliver & Company

FRIENDS IN NEED

The orphaned kitten left alone in New York City didn't stand much of a chance. But a streetwise dog named Dodger had taken pity on the poor kitten.

The kitten was thankful to the dog. Dodger had protected him from vicious Dobermans and took him on

board the old barge, where he lived as part of the gang.

Tito, Einstein and Rita were glad to have a new friend,

and the master of the boat, Fagin, had been kind and

gentle, reading a story while petting the kitten in his lap.

Happily the kitten curled up next to Dodger for the

night. As the dog watched the kitten sleeping beside him, he felt a protective bond and smiled tenderly at his new friend.

The next day the group set out to help Fagin. The

poor man owed money to a gangster named Sykes, and the loyal dogs would do whatever they could to lend a paw. They decided to split up to do their work and

Dodger told Tito the Chihuahua to keep his eye on the kitten.

The kitten was ready for adventure and followed Tito into an expensive car. As the Chihuahua tried to remove the car stereo, the kitten jumped onto the dashboard nervously, hitting the horn and blasting Tito out.

The terrified kitten tried to hide, but a little girl named

Jenny leaned over from the back seat to comfort him. As
she cuddled him, the kitten felt happier than he ever had
before. "I'm going to take you home," she promised.

Lovingly, Jenny carried the kitten into her fancy Fifth

Avenue apartment. She named him Oliver and made him
a special meal, promising, "I'll take good care of you."

Together they played and practised piano. Jenny
bought Oliver a beautiful silver bowl and a collar with
a shiny name tag. She had been upset when her parents

said they wouldn't be home for her birthday, but now she wasn't lonely anymore. Oliver was her new friend.

At school the next day Jenny felt excited about the kitten waiting for her at home. Little did she know that Dodger and the gang were sneaking him out of the house

while she
was away.

Proud of their
rescue, Dodger let
Oliver out of the
bag when they
returned to the
boat. "You're home

now," he told the kitten proudly. Oliver wasn't pleased. "I

was happy there," he said sadly. "I want to go back."

Dodger felt crushed and reacted angrily. "Leave then!"

he said harshly, nodding towards the side of the boat.

Oliver was sorry that he had hurt his friend, but knew he

belonged with Jenny. Apologetically, he started to leave

when Fagin appeared. Noticing Oliver's expensive name

tag, the desperate man came up with an idea to ransom

the kitten in the
hope of exchanging
Oliver for the
money he needed
to pay his debt to
Sykes.

Unfortunately,
Jenny received the
note. The heartbroken little girl set out to find Oliver.
With her vain and spoiled dog, Georgette, at her side, she
carried her piggy bank and followed the map Fagin had
written. Eventually Jenny found her way to the boat.

"I'm trying to get my kitten back," she told Fagin.

Feeling ashamed, he returned Oliver to her, but at that moment Sykes drove up in his black limousine. The little girl was worth more money than the kitten, he thought, pulling her through the window.

Oliver was distraught. "We'll get her back," promised Dodger. Teaming up, the group made a daring rescue, escaping from Sykes' warehouse with Jenny.

However, the evil man's car was faster than Fagin's three-wheeled motorbike. Sykes caught Jenny by the hand, but Oliver courageously jumped onto the car and bit him.

Fagin saved the little girl and Dodger leaped to

protect Oliver, and
fought the
Dobermans in the
back of the
limousine.

Finally the chase
ended when Sykes'
car sped off an
unfinished bridge. Dodger and Oliver jumped off just in
time. Quickly, Fagin returned to get them, but as Jenny
lifted Oliver he was unconscious. They all looked
sorrowfully at the brave kitten just as he opened his eyes.

"Oliver!" cried Jenny swinging him around joyfully. The little girl embraced the kitten happily as he purred in her arms. When Jenny celebrated her birthday she invited all her animal friends, and Fagin, too. They had a party fit for a princess.

DISNEY'S

TARZAN®

You'll Always Be in My Heart

Young Tarzan looked with anguish at his reflection in the water and covered his face with mud. He desperately wanted to fit in with the other gorillas. Why am I different? he thought. He wanted to look like the rest of his family. He wanted to move as surely through

the trees and be as strong, too.

When his mother, Kala, found him, she felt his pain. Trying to comfort Tarzan, she showed him that they had the same hands and that her heartbeat was the same as his. Enveloped in his mother's hug, the boy felt a new strength and determination. "I'll be the best ape ever!" he promised.

True to his word, Tarzan grew into an adult with great

skills. He imitated the jungle animals and wrestled with his best friend, Terk, until he developed ways to overcome her superior strength. He swung from trees with great speed. With a spear he had invented, he was even able to rescue Kerchak, the gorilla leader, from the vicious leopard, Sabor.

Proudly, he earned acceptance from his peers. Up until the day he met Jane, Tarzan had put his doubts and miseries behind him.

When gunshots rang out one day, Tarzan investigated the strange noise. He was surprised to come upon three strange creatures. Clayton, a hunter, was leading Professor Porter and his daughter, Jane, on an expedition to study gorillas.

When Jane stayed behind to sketch a young baboon, Tarzan rescued her from the baboon's angry family. After the terrifying chase, Jane tried to back away from the wild man, but he came closer to her, touching her hands with a look of fascination. They were just like his! When he listened to her heartbeat and laid her head against his

own chest, she was afraid, but she realised that he wasn't

going to hurt her. Though his eyes were intense, his smile

was kind and his manner gentle.

"Tarzan," he spoke, pointing to himself, and they began

to communicate. Slowly, Tarzan learned Jane's language.

Visiting the human camp, he was fascinated by pictures of

people and places.

Everything was new to

Tarzan. Jane and her

father, excited by his

enthusiasm, became

Tarzan's teachers.

"I've never seen him so happy," said Tarzan's friends, as they watched him pick flowers for Jane. He could not stop thinking about her. The bond between them had become more than a simple attraction. One morning, Tarzan arrived at the campsite but was surprised to learn that it was time for Jane to leave.

"Jane. Stay!" pleaded Tarzan as he handed her some

flowers. Jane cried and ran away. She was as upset as Tarzan about leaving.

Nearby, Clayton was forming a wicked plan. Wanting to capture the gorillas, he made Tarzan believe that Jane might stay if she could meet the apes.

Jane and her father were thrilled when Tarzan brought them to his family. Joyfully, Jane watched Tarzan talking to the young gorillas. "Can you teach me?" Jane asked.

Gently, Tarzan helped her form the gorilla words. As the apes reacted noisily, Jane wanted to know what he had taught her to say. "Jane stays with Tarzan," he told her, but she shook her head.

That evening Tarzan sat in a tree watching the distant boat anchored offshore. He wasn't sure what he should

do. Kala had told him he was her son, but he looked like the humans. Where did he belong?

Kala joined Tarzan in the tree. Silently she led him to the tree house where she had found him years ago. An old picture of his human family was still on the floor. "I just want you to be happy . . . whatever you decide," she told him.

Moments later, he had dressed in his father's clothes. "No matter where I go you will always be my mother," said Tarzan to Kala as he headed towards the beach. "And you will always be in my heart," she replied.

Tarzan's friends

Tantor and Terk watched sadly as the ship pulled away.

Moments later a wild cry of despair reached the shore.

Tarzan was in trouble! Clayton had locked him in the

hold – he had an evil plan to capture the apes and take

them back in cages on the ship. Once home he planned to sell them.

Quickly the friends swam to the ship. Bravely fighting off Clayton's men, they released Tarzan and Jane. "I thought I was never going to see you again!" sobbed Tantor.

Calling the jungle animals for help, they fought Clayton and his men, but Kerchak, the gorilla leader, was shot

trying to save Tarzan. "Forgive me for not understanding that you have always been one of us," the dying gorilla told Tarzan. "Take care of our family . . . my son."

Even though she had said a tearful good-bye to Tarzan, once, Jane realised that she loved him too much to leave.

Splashing back to shore from the boat, she embraced him joyfully, as friends and family cheered. "Oo-oo-ee-eh-ou," said Jane. "Jane stays with Tarzan!"